ANDREW CLEMENTS

The Handiest Things in the World

Photographs by Raquel Jaramillo

atheneum books for young readers · New York · London · Toronto · Sydney

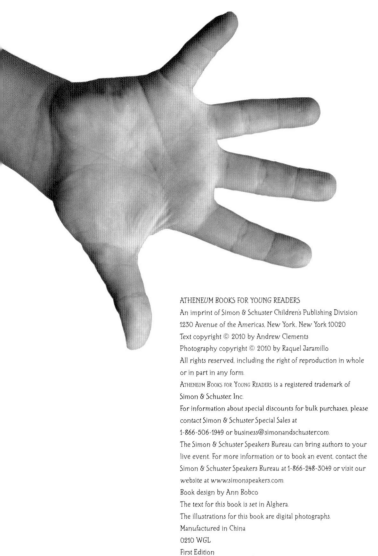

ATHENEUM BOOKS FOR YOUNG READERS

An imprint of Simon & Schuster Children's Publishing Division

1230 Avenue of the Americas, New York, New York 10020

Text copyright © 2010 by Andrew Clements

Photography copyright © 2010 by Raquel Jaramillo

All rights reserved, including the right of reproduction in whole

or in part in any form.

ATHENEUM BOOKS FOR YOUNG READERS is a registered trademark of

Simon & Schuster, Inc.

For information about special discounts for bulk purchases, please

contact Simon & Schuster Special Sales at

1-866-506-1949 or business@simonandschuster.com.

The Simon & Schuster Speakers Bureau can bring authors to your

live event. For more information or to book an event, contact the

Simon & Schuster Speakers Bureau at 1-866-248-3049 or visit our

website at www.simonspeakers.com.

Book design by Ann Bobco

The text for this book is set in Alghera.

The illustrations for this book are digital photographs.

Manufactured in China

0210 WGL

First Edition

10 9 8 7 6 5 4 3 2 1

CIP data for this book is available from the Library of Congress.

ISBN: 978-1-4169-6166-6

For John and Kristen

—A. C.

For Russell, who makes all things possible

—R. J.

Acknowledgments: Thanks to Allie, Bella, Ella, Jessie, Raimi, Carter, Marshall, Brody, Elise, Marco, Gallie, Owen, Taylor, Nate, Julia, Sarah, Ben, Jake, and Lucas for the exquisite use of their hands—and to their moms and dads for the many lovely weekends they sacrificed in the making of this book. A million thanks to Caleb, for being the world's best photographer's assistant. And a special mighty THANK-YOU to Josey, without whose small, beautiful hands this book could not have been made. —R. J.

Of all the handy things there are,
the hand itself is best by far.
To grab, to hold, to pull or twist—
the hand itself is handiest.

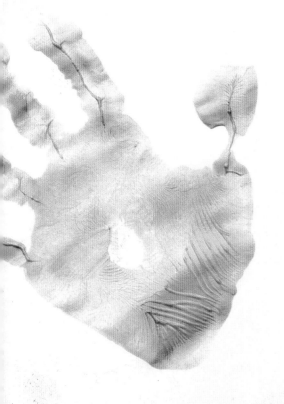

But other things are handy, too.
Just look around, you'll see it's true.
Which things are handiest for you?
Depends on what you need to do.

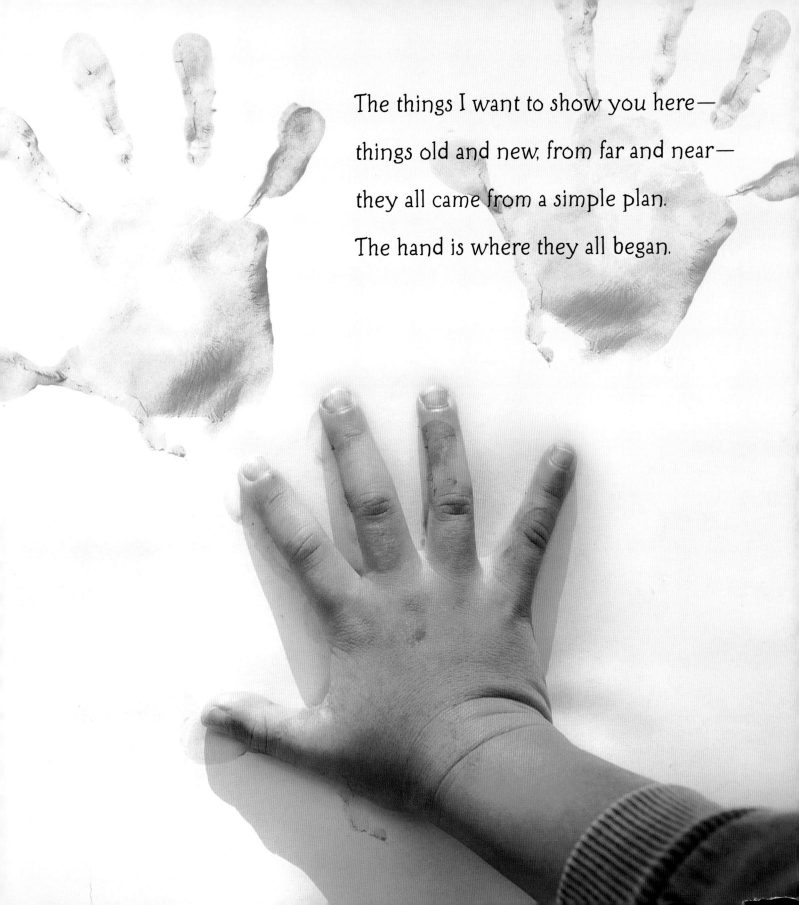

The things I want to show you here—
things old and new, from far and near—
they all came from a simple plan.
The hand is where they all began.

Mealtime happens
every day.

Keep your fingers clean this way.

Don't let Rover stray away.

This will hold him night and day.

...five, six, seven, eight, nine, ten.

Add, subtract, then add again.

Zig-zag,
flit-flap —
hard to get.

Catch him with your handy net.

Two wet hands
can hold
and pour.

This will pour a whole lot more.

Raindrops falling
from the sky.

This will help to keep you dry.

Wish I might, wish I may . . .

sweep
this dusty stuff
away.

Handmade
shade
for
squinty
eyes.

This
will help
with
sunny
skies.

Digging in and scooping down.

Let's move lots of dirt around.

Tidy
is the way
to be.

This will help enormously.

Flap
a hand
to make a
breeze.

Push more air
with
one of these.

Tap in rhythm,
keep
the
beat.

Work with these and make some heat.

What's the width,
or length, or height?

This
thing
always
gets
it right.

Sticky fingers make a mess.

Mixers
make
the mess
much
less.

Waves
will
wash
these
words

AWAY

Write
this way,
and words
will

When windy wintertime appears . . .

these feel
good on
frosty ears.

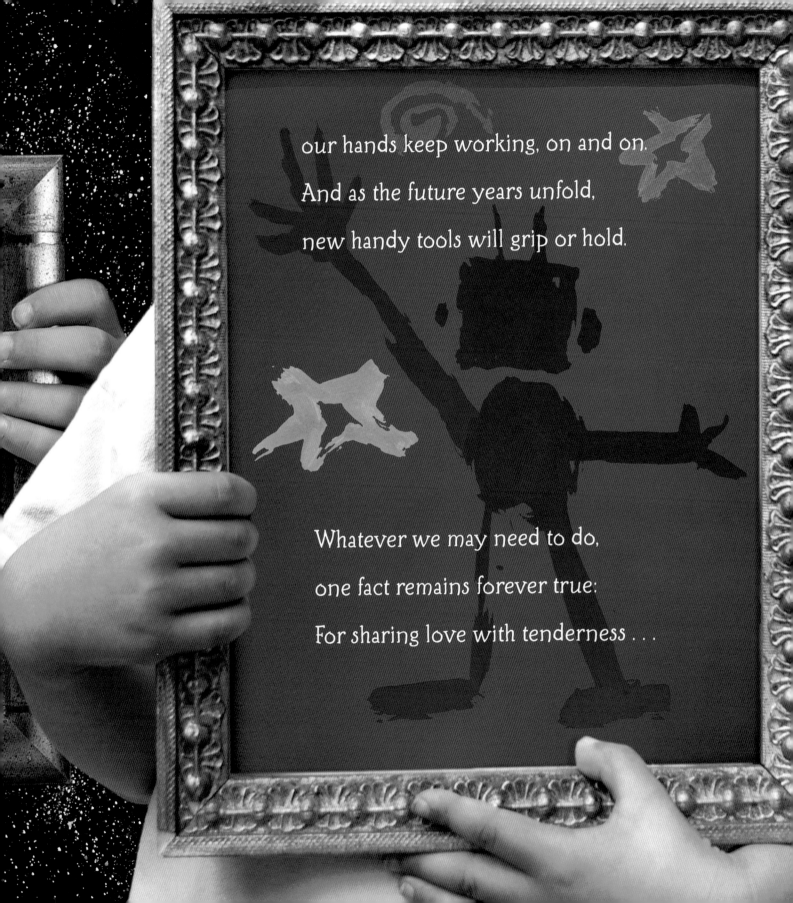

our hands keep working, on and on.

And as the future years unfold,

new handy tools will grip or hold.

Whatever we may need to do,

one fact remains forever true:

For sharing love with tenderness . . .

the hand itself

is handiest.